Deadly Threats

THE
LIGHT CHASER MYSTERIES
3

DEADLY
THREATS

HORIZON BOOKS
CAMP HILL, PENNSYLVANIA

Dedicated to
Mr. Joe Tewinkel
of Crown College

Horizon Books
3825 Hartzdale Drive
Camp Hill, PA 17011

ISBN: 0-88965-108-6
LOC Catalog Card Number: 94-78636
© 1995 by Mark Weinrich
All rights reserved
Printed in the United States of America

Cover Art © by Gary Watson

95 96 97 98 99   5   4   3   2   1

Book 3 of the Light Chaser™ Mystery Series

Preface

Few stories have stirred my imagination as much as the Oscar Willett story. Since I first read about it in 1985, I have wanted to use it in a book. I want to thank Deb Davis of Superior, Montana, for her permission to use portions of her newspaper article about Oscar Willett.

The character Gabriel Flores, his family and the letter from Oscar Willett are all fiction. No one in the town of Monticello has treated anyone the way Gabriel Flores was treated in this book.

Many sick people before the advent of modern medicine were misunderstood and mistreated. Because of ignorance and superstition many endured inhumane conditions and ultimately died rejected and alone.

I hope this book will challenge Christians to treat others the way Jesus would have treated them.

1

The Threat

Steam rose in a small cloud when Rainie Trevors opened the dishwasher door. "There's something in that cave," Rainie said, "and someone doesn't want us to find out what it is."

"Caves aren't any place to mess around," Aunt Amie said as she rolled her wheelchair closer to the dishwasher.

Rainie slid out a rack of dishes and started unloading glasses and putting them in the cupboard. Sometimes Rainie thought Aunt Amie worried too much about her and her brother, Ryan. She was thirteen and Ryan eleven. Aunt Amie hadn't said anything about Ryan helping Uncle Matt work cattle this week. And working cattle could be dangerous, too. "We can at least check the cave out, can't we? Besides, Denise is going to be here anytime, and Uncle Matt thought it would be okay."

"I don't know if I want you involved in this mystery." Aunt Amie started sorting silverware and putting it away. "I don't think threats are a thing to take lightly."

Rainie flipped her brown hair back over her shoulders; it kept falling in her face when she bent over to pick up the dishes. She wished she hadn't told her aunt about the threat. "There's only been one threat so far, and it might just be a joke."

"Go home or else," Aunt Amie said, "isn't my idea of a joke." She turned her wheelchair around and left the kitchen.

For some reason Aunt Amie was upset about Rainie and Denise going to the cave. Rainie kept unloading the breakfast dishes. She wanted to get her chores done before Denise arrived. Maybe she could talk to Aunt Amie this afternoon.

Two days before, Rainie and her sixteen-year-old friend Denise Rodriquez had attended a meeting at Geronimo Springs Museum. When they returned to Denise's pickup after the meeting, the right front tire was flat, and someone had scratched "Go home or else" in the dust over the fender.

Whoever had let the air out of the tire was either playing a joke or trying to scare them. But the words "go home" were meant for Rainie. Someone wanted her to go back to Pennsylvania. Since she and her brother, Ryan, had come to their aunt and uncle's ranch in New Mexico the month before, she had solved two mysteries.

After the threat at Geronimo Springs, Denise and Rainie had discussed why anyone would threaten Rainie.

"I think we're close to solving another mystery," Rainie said.

"But what?" Denise responded.

"We obviously stumbled on to something that caused someone to worry."

"Maybe it has something to do with the Monticello light," Denise suggested.

When Denise had mentioned the Monticello light, Rainie remembered the hike she and Denise had taken three weeks before. They had been trying to figure out why a mysterious light occasionally appeared over the town of Monticello.

Rainie had never seen the light, but Denise said it looked spooky. An eerie light with a greenish glow hung low almost over the post office. Some people claimed it was a yard light turned skyward instead of toward the ground, but no one had been able to figure out exactly what it was.

While searching for the source of the light, Denise and Rainie had found two caves in the hills north of Monticello. Both caves were just over-hangs—ledges of rock sticking out of the hills where a person could seek shelter. But one had been bricked in with adobe bricks. Why would anyone take the time to wall in the cave?

Animals had dug around the bottom of the left

side of the adobe wall and created a hole that
Rainie thought she could squeeze through. But if
she crawled in the hole, the light would be blocked
out. She and Denise had agreed to come back with
flashlights, but then they had been caught up in
another mystery and forgotten the cave until the
evening they received the threat.

When Rainie finished emptying the dishwasher,
she peered into Aunt Amie's office and heard the
clicking of the computer keyboard. Aunt Amie
was writing, so maybe she wasn't too upset. Rainie
stopped by the office door. Uncle Matt had already
said she could go. Well, Denise wasn't here yet, so
she'd better not put it off. Something was bother-
ing Aunt Amie. Rainie knocked on the door.

"Come in," Aunt Amie called.

"Excuse me," Rainie said as she peeked in the
door.

"Just a minute," answered Aunt Amie. She typed
with her left hand and held a pencil in her right
hand to hold down the shift key.

Rainie was surprised by all that Aunt Amie
could do in spite of having multiple sclerosis.
Uncle Matt and Aunt Amie had served for twenty-
three years as missionaries in Africa, but they had
been forced to return to America because of Aunt
Amie's illness. Now Uncle Matt ran the Warm
Springs Ranch which he had inherited from his
brother, and Aunt Amie wrote Christian mysteries
for adults. Rainie had just finished reading one of
her aunt's books. She couldn't wait to read more.

"How's your new book coming?" Rainie asked.

"Slower than I'd like." Aunt Amie punched a few more keys, then turned and smiled. "I guess it doesn't help having a couple of kids around."

"We love having you," replied Aunt Amie, "and we're going to miss you."

Rainie and her younger brother, Ryan, had been sent out to visit their aunt and uncle while their mother finished nursing school. Rainie didn't want to think about going back. Only two weeks remained until they had to go home.

"I wanted to talk to you about today." Rainie wrung her hands nervously.

"I'm sorry if I was short with you this morning," Aunt Amie said, "but I'm afraid things may get out of hand with your mysteries."

"What do you mean?" Rainie looked down at her hands.

"When you encounter conflict like this threat you've received, it generally means one of two things. Either you are going in the wrong direction and God has put a roadblock to slow you down, or Satan is opposing what you are trying to do. What kind of conflict do you think you're encountering?"

Rainie looked up into Aunt Amie's hard brown eyes. She wasn't smiling anymore. "I think it must be Satan," said Rainie.

"I believe you're right."

"Then what's wrong?" Rainie almost burst out.

"You've been treating these mysteries like a game. I believe what you are doing now is deadly serious."

The doorbell rang.

"That must be Denise," Rainie said and turned to the door.

"She can wait a minute," Aunt Amie commanded.

"Just a minute!" Rainie yelled toward the hall.

"If it wasn't for Denise," Aunt Amie said, "I wouldn't let you do this."

"Can I go?"

"First, let me pray with you."

Rainie knelt next to her aunt, and they held hands. Aunt Amie prayed that God would protect them and keep them safe.

When Rainie turned to leave, Aunt Amie said, "Remember to do all that your uncle told you to."

"I will." She hugged Aunt Amie. "Thank you, I'll be careful."

Rainie ran down the hall, grabbed Uncle Matt's day pack and flashlights and raced out the door.

Denise was leaning against her pickup when Rainie came out the back door. But Denise wasn't alone. A strange guy was leaning next to Denise with his arm across her shoulders.

Rainie slowed to a walk. What now? she thought.

2

The Dungeon

"Rainie, this is Kerry Reese," Denise said. "I hope you don't mind that he's coming today."

Kerry took off his black cowboy hat and held out his hand. "I'm pleased to meet you." His hair was almost as dark as his hat. His T-shirt read "State Championship Basketball Tournament." It was obvious he played basketball; he looked like he was a couple of inches over six feet. He was almost as tall as Uncle Matt.

Rainie tried to smile as she shook Kerry's hand. "I guess it's okay. You're driving." Then she wished she hadn't said that. Denise probably thought she was angry.

Kerry opened the pickup door and slid into the middle of the seat. Rainie walked around the truck, opened the other door, threw the pack on the floorboard, then climbed in next to Kerry.

"I just thought we might need some help," Denise said when she started the truck. "Kerry's been on vacation the last few weeks."

"Where'd you go?" Rainie asked, trying to be a little more friendly.

"I went to visit my grandparents in Montana," Kerry said.

"What's Montana like?" Rainie asked.

"Really green compared to this," Kerry said, pointing to the desert landscape as they passed. "But I missed this."

"How could you miss this?" Denise exclaimed.

"I guess because it's home," Kerry said. "If I want to see green, all I have to do is go to the mountains." Then he pointed to the blue-green expanse of the San Mateo Mountains rising to the north.

"Do you miss Pennsylvania?" Denise asked Rainie.

"Not really," Rainie said. "I miss Mom, but I hate to think about going back."

"Why?" Denise asked.

"Because I'm going to miss Uncle Matt and Aunt Amie." Rainie didn't want to admit it, but being with Uncle Matt and Aunt Amie was like being at home. She never imagined her aunt and uncle's Warm Springs Ranch would seem so much like home.

They drove several miles in silence. Rainie was absorbed in thoughts of home.

"What do you think is in the cave?" Kerry asked and broke the silence.

Rainie felt irritated. Denise had probably told him everything. "I don't have any idea," Rainie said. "I just think someone doesn't want us to find out what's in it."

"Do you think it has anything to do with the Monticello light?" Kerry asked.

Rainie sighed. Denise had told him everything. "I guess we'll try and find out," Rainie answered.

Denise turned left up a gravel road instead of taking the pavement into Monticello.

"Where are we going?" Rainie asked.

"I thought it would be easier to follow the ridge down to the cave than it would be climbing up," Denise said.

The road followed the edge of the hill. The hilltop rose just above them now. Denise pulled over into a turnout. A trail ran up the bank to the hilltop.

They scrambled up the trail to the hilltop. The town of Monticello looked incredibly small from this view. The spire of the old Catholic church stuck out on the left, and then a few houses were visible through the tall cottonwood trees.

"Not very big, is it?" Kerry said.

"No," Denise said, "but it's big enough."

Rainie felt the same way. She really didn't want to go back to city life.

As they looked around, they could see that the ridge split into three fingers.

"From up here," Rainie said, "the hill looks like a giant bird track."

"You're right," Kerry said. "It looks like a big turkey track."

"Where do we go from here?" Rainie asked.

"I'll show you," Denise said. "I've only been up here once before, and that was just playing around when I was younger."

The caves were between the toes of the giant track. From the base of the middle toe they could look down at the bricked-over cave on the left and the exposed overhang on their right. Denise led them down the middle toe of the bird track and then back up between the second and third toe.

"Why would anyone completely seal over a cave?" Kerry asked.

"That's what we're going to find out," Rainie said as she placed her pack on a large flat rock next to where something had made a hole in the bottom of the wall. The hole looked much smaller than she remembered. Rainie took a flashlight from her pack.

"You'd better check for snakes," Denise said, "before you crawl in there."

"I know," Rainie said. "Uncle Matt told me to throw rocks in."

"Better yet," Kerry said, "use this." He broke the woody stem of a yucca plant and handed it to Rainie.

Rainie got on her knees and tried to throw a rock sidearm. The rock bounced in the dirt barely inside the cave.

"Here, let me," Kerry said. He knelt and threw several rocks in the hole.

"I don't think it's very deep," he said. "I think I hit the back wall."

"If there was a rattler in there," Denise said, "he would've buzzed by now."

"Buzzed?" Rainie asked.

"You mean you haven't seen a rattlesnake yet?" Kerry said as he reached for the yucca stick. He probed inside the hole with the stick, trying to reach as far as he could.

"When a rattlesnake rattles, it makes a buzzing sound," Denise said. "You'll know when you hear one the first time. You'll want to jump out of your skin."

"I don't think there're any snakes in here," Kerry said.

Rainie breathed deeply. She didn't realize she'd been holding her breath. She hated snakes.

"Do you want me to climb in the hole first?" Kerry asked.

"No," Rainie said, "we need to do one more thing. Uncle Matt said to make sure the wall is stable before we crawl in."

"That's right," Kerry said. "Sometimes you can push these walls over; they're so unstable."

"Plus, I wouldn't want that wall to fall in on me," Denise said.

The mud bricks of the adobe wall were rough, and the outside surface crumbled to the touch.

Rain melted these mud walls over the years unless they were plastered. The overhang had protected most of the wall except in places where the rain blew in.

Kerry leaned with his weight against the wall. "It doesn't give."

"Try by the hole," Rainie said.

"It feels solid."

"Okay. Here goes." Rainie grabbed her flashlight and crawled headfirst into the hole. "Ouch. Remind me to wear gloves and long sleeves next time. There are cactus needles on the floor."

Now that she was part way through the opening, her body blocked any sunlight from getting into the hole. She turned on her flashlight and crawled all the way in. "Well, it's not big. It's about eight feet deep by twelve or fifteen wide."

"Can you see anything yet?" Denise yelled.

Rainie stood up. "No, not yet, but it's sure dusty in here." She took her flashlight and started searching systematically from the hole to the right. The cave was like a walk-in closet except for the dirt floor.

"Are you all right?" Kerry asked.

"No problem," Rainie called back. "Wait, there's something hanging from the wall. It's some kind of a chain."

"We're coming in," Denise called.

"It's a pretty tight squeeze," Rainie called back. She followed the chain to the wall. A large bolt fastened it to the wall.

The sunlight from the hole was blocked as Kerry crawled through. "Hand me a flashlight," Kerry said to Denise.

"Ouch," Kerry said when he bumped his head on the ceiling.

"Sorry," Rainie said. "I didn't have any problem, so I didn't think to warn you. Come, look at this."

"Wait, you two," Denise called.

They waited, and when Denise joined them, Rainie traced the chain to the wall and showed them the bolt. Then she began pulling at the rest of the chain that was buried in the floor. About six feet of chain came loose from beneath the dusty floor.

"There's something on the end of it," Denise said.

They pointed the beam of their flashlights at the free end of the chain. A metal ring was attached with a hole where a lock could hold it together.

"Someone or something was locked in here," Rainie said.

"Yeah. This is like a dungeon!" Kerry exclaimed.

"But why would anyone chain someone in here?" Denise asked.

"That's what we're going to find out," Rainie said, excitement filling her voice.

3

Second Threat

"Boy, it sure is dusty in here," Denise said with a cough.

"Uh huh. I feel like I can't breathe," choked Rainie. "We'd better get out of here. Then maybe the dust will settle." She held her hand over her mouth in an effort to keep out the dust and to keep from choking.

One at a time they squeezed back out through the opening.

"That's worse than a chicken coop," Kerry said after they crawled out.

Rainie took a couple of deep breaths. "Fresh air is wonderful," she said.

"I can't believe something was locked in there," Denise commented.

"I think it was someone," Rainie said. "The chain is too short for any kind of animal, and the ring on the end is just the right size for a person's ankle or wrist. The real question is when?"

"What are you getting at?" Kerry asked.

"How long ago do you think someone did this?" Rainie pointed at the cave.

"I'm pretty sure it hasn't been recent," Kerry said as he grabbed his hat from the flat rock and put it on. "The adobe looks real old."

"That doesn't mean anything," Denise explained. "People often take adobe bricks from old buildings and use them again."

"One thing is certain," Rainie said. "Someone is trying to hide something. I'm sure the wall was built after whoever or whatever was chained here left."

"How do you know that?" Kerry asked.

"She's right. There's no door," Denise said.

"You two are amazing," Kerry said, "but you've had more experience." Then he looked at Rainie and spoke in a deep, mysterious voice, "I'll catch up with you, Sherlock." Then he glanced at Denise, "And you, Dr. Watson."

The girls laughed.

"But who does that make you?" Denise asked and winked at Rainie.

"Mrs. Hudson," Rainie said, trying to fake a British accent.

Both the girls laughed again as they sat down in the shade cast by the overhang.

Kerry sat down next to them. "Who's Mrs. Hudson?" he asked.

The girls just kept laughing.

Kerry shook his head. "Girls," he said in disgust.

"I guess you haven't read too many Sherlock Holmes mysteries," Denise said, smiling at Rainie.

"Mrs. Hudson was Sherlock's housekeeper," Rainie said.

Kerry took off his hat and raised it like he was going to hit the girls, and then he burst out laughing.

"I think it's time for tea," Rainie said with her British accent. "Mrs. Hudson, could you pass me my pack?"

Kerry raised Rainie's pack as if he was going to throw it at her, and then just handed it to her.

Rainie opened the pack, took out a canteen and passed it to the others.

"Are we going to go back in?" Denise asked after taking a drink. She passed the canteen to Rainie.

Rainie took a drink and said, "I don't know yet. I just had a thought about what the cave might have been used for. Have you read *Old Yeller*?"

Denise nodded.

Kerry smiled. "My fourth grade teacher read it to us in class."

"Do you remember when Old Yeller got rabies?" Rainie asked.

"They had to shoot him," Denise replied.

Rainie leaned forward and started drawing in the dirt with a stick. "Remember earlier in the story when one of the neighbors brought the news that there was an outbreak of rabies in the area?

Then he told the story about one of his relatives who had rabies."

"I remember," Kerry said. "He was chained to a tree until he died."

"What if something like that happened here?" Rainie asked as she put the stick down. "I don't think we should go back in until we investigate some more."

"Why?" Denise asked.

"Do you remember when the cow got rabies in *Old Yeller*?" Rainie asked.

"They shot it, then buried the carcass under a pile of wood and burned it," Kerry responded. "That was when Old Yeller fought the wolf and got rabies."

"So, if someone died of rabies in this cave," Denise said, "they were trying to protect people from the disease. That's why they walled it off."

"Great!" Kerry exclaimed. "And we've been messing around in there."

No one spoke. Rainie picked up the stick and drew in the dirt again.

"What do we do now?" Denise asked.

"What we should have done before we went in the cave," Rainie said.

"What?" Denise asked.

"Pray," Rainie said.

Kerry took off his hat. Rainie prayed, "Father, I believe You have led us here. Please protect us. We give this problem to You. In Jesus' name, Amen."

They were silent again.

"Praise God," Rainie said, "I just got an idea."

Denise and Kerry looked at her with questioning glances.

"It wouldn't have to be rabies," Rainie said. "It could be any one of a number of diseases. Years ago if people had epilepsy or some other disease that was incurable, their families locked them up and acted as if the person was dead."

"Phew," Kerry said, breathing a sigh of relief. "I was thinking about those rabies shots. I've heard they give you a shot in the stomach."

"It's a series of shots in the stomach," Denise said.

"Thanks for the good news," Kerry replied.

"Forget rabies for a minute," Rainie said. "Years ago mentally ill people were treated the same way. It was often kept a secret. People didn't want anyone to know they had a crazy person in the family."

"That sounds like the best idea yet," Kerry said.

"We'd better go," Denise said. She looked at Rainie and added, "Maybe your Aunt Amie will be able to help us figure this out."

Rainie put the canteen back in the pack, and then they started on the trail back. They stopped on the top of the ridge where they could look down on the bricked-over cave, now shrouded in shade.

"It's hard to notice," Rainie said. "You'd have to be up here at just the right time of day to see it."

"I'm surprised you found it," Kerry said. "Aren't you, Dr. Watson?"

"Sherlock doesn't miss much," Denise said. "How about Mrs. Hudson?"

"She . . . he is learning," Kerry sputtered.

The girls laughed as they started back up the ridge.

Kerry followed and mumbled, "Girls."

When they reached the pickup Denise screamed, "Oh no! My dad is going to kill me!"

Kerry and Rainie followed Denise's gaze. The passenger side door of the pickup had been bashed in.

"Wow. We really do have enemies," said Rainie.

"I'd say so," said Kerry. "We can get it fixed, but your dad sure won't be too happy."

"Look!" Rainie pointed at the dust above where the door had been kicked in. "Quit Snooping" had been scratched in the dust.

4

Good and Bad News

After Denise and Kerry left, Rainie sat at the dining room table visiting with Aunt Amie. Rainie wished they were still here. She knew Aunt Amie was concerned about the second threat, but she hadn't said anything yet.

"Kerry seems to be a nice young man," Aunt Amie said.

Rainie drew lines with her finger in the sweat of her iced tea glass. "He seems fine," Rainie said.

"I'm sorry if I came down too hard on you this morning," Aunt Amie said. "If I were your age, I would love to be doing what you have been doing. But I still think you're just treating these mysteries like games."

"I know these threats are serious," Rainie said, "and if we don't find out what these people are hiding, somebody else will, sooner or later."

"Maybe you're not the one to solve this mystery," Aunt Amie suggested.

"Then why would the Lord have allowed me to find the cave in the first place?" Rainie asked.

"I don't know," Aunt Amie said, "but we're responsible for you while you're here. The door of a truck is a lot easier to fix than an injured life. And with everything else you've told me, I don't know that you should continue with this mystery."

"Can we talk about this some more before you make a decision?" Rainie asked.

"We'll talk about it some more when your uncle gets home." Aunt Amie rolled her wheelchair backward and then turned toward the counter that divided the kitchen and dining room. "With all this mystery talk, I forgot to give this to you." She reached up and picked a letter off the counter.

"From Mom?" Rainie asked.

Aunt Amie smiled and nodded.

Rainie grabbed the letter and almost tore it open. This was only the second letter that they'd received since they'd been there. Mom called every Saturday night, so this had to be something special.

Dear Rainie and Ryan,

I hope this will be wonderful news for you. At least, I think it is wonderful.

Aunt Amie sent me a clipping from the Geronimo Springs newspaper about some nursing jobs at the hospital in Geronimo Springs. I will be flying out in two weeks to interview for the job. There is a good chance that we could live in New Mexico permanently. Wouldn't it be great to live so close to Uncle Matt and Aunt Amie?

"What does it say?" Aunt Amie asked. "You're beaming all over."

"Mom says she's flying out in two weeks. She might be able to get that nursing job you wrote her about," Rainie answered. Then she continued reading.

"That would be nice. How do you think Ryan's going to react?" Aunt Amie asked.

Rainie didn't respond. She just sat still, staring at the letter.

Slowly the paper slipped from Rainie's hand and fell to the floor. She burst into tears.

"What's wrong?" asked Aunt Amie.

Rainie bent down, picked up the letter and handed it to Aunt Amie. Then she put her elbows on the table with her head in her hands while Aunt Amie read the bad news.

I don't know how to share what I heard this week. At first, I thought it was a rumor, so I called Jennifer Warren's mom to make sure it was the truth. Jennifer has been diagnosed with HIV.

I know you two haven't been as close late-

ly, but I thought you ought to know so you
could contact her.

When Jennifer was little, she had a blood
transfusion. It must have been AIDS-tainted
blood.

I guess they've known for quite a while,
but they've been afraid to tell anyone for
fear of how the community would react.
Lately Jennifer has been sick a lot. Somehow someone found out, and now the
whole community knows.

Pray for Jennifer and her family. I'm so
sorry to have to share this with you. I'm
praying for you. I can't wait to see you.

Love,
Mom

"How close are you to Jennifer?" Aunt Amie
asked.

"We used to be best friends," Rainie said, looking up through red eyes, "but since I accepted the
Lord, we haven't been very close. She didn't want
to come to church with me. We just kind of grew
apart."

"I'm so sorry, Rainie." Aunt Amie reached out
for Rainie's hand.

Rainie grabbed Aunt Amie's hand and started to
sob again. "Why?" she said. "Why did this have to
happen?"

"Sometimes we will never know until we stand

before the Lord," Aunt Amie replied. "I would be lying if I tried to answer. All I know is that God promises to work all things for good to those that love Him. That doesn't mean that all things *are* good, but He will work all things together for good."

"How could God work this together for good?"

"Well, I know in my life sometimes God has to use difficulties or problems to get my attention. It's during those dark, hard times that I see how much I need God and how much He really does care about me. Maybe Jennifer will feel the same way. Maybe she'll come to know the Lord." Aunt Amie gently squeezed Rainie's hand.

Rainie looked up. "Oh, I hope so."

Rainie couldn't sleep that night. She kept thinking about Jennifer. At supper she'd barely shared anything about the cave with Uncle Matt and Ryan.

Ryan had surprised Rainie. He almost yelled for joy when he heard about the possibility of moving to New Mexico.

Rainie felt hurt that Jennifer hadn't said anything to her about her problem. Why hadn't Jennifer told her? She thought back over the past. Then Rainie remembered the assembly at school last fall. A guy with AIDS had been the speaker. Just listening to what he said almost made her sick. After the assembly many of the other kids shook hands with the guy. Now Jennifer's reaction to him made sense. She had hugged him.

But Rainie had just stood in the auditorium aisle and waited for Jennifer. Then Jennifer had cried on their walk home from school. Rainie thought it was sympathy for the guy with AIDS. Now she knew. Now she wished she had shaken his hand. Maybe then Jennifer would have told her that she had HIV.

She tried to sleep, but she just couldn't get comfortable. Why did she feel this way?

She slipped from bed to her knees. *Father, forgive me. Jennifer needs You now more than ever. Show me what to do. Help me to be a better friend.*

5

More Questions

Rainie groaned and rolled over in bed, wrapping the covers around herself. She felt like she had just gone to sleep. Who was knocking on her door?

"Rainie, Rainie," Uncle Matt called from behind the bedroom door. "Get up and come here. I need to talk with you."

It wasn't even light yet. She strained to read her watch. It looked like it read 4 a.m. What did Uncle Matt want?

She grabbed her robe and staggered out into the hall. The smell of coffee hung in the air.

Uncle Matt and Ryan sat on one side of the dining room table, and Cinch, one of Uncle Matt's ranch hands, sat on the other. A map was spread out between them. It looked like they were planning something.

"What's this I hear? We might get stuck with you two moving here for good," Cinch said. Rainie could tell Cinch was smiling, but only by the way the edges of his waterfall mustache raised at the corners of his mouth.

"We're not sure yet," Rainie said. "What's going on?"

"We're going to help you with your mystery," Ryan said.

"I thought you weren't going to let me," Rainie said, looking at Uncle Matt.

"I talked with Denise's parents on the phone last night," Uncle Matt said, "and we've changed our minds."

"Even Aunt Amie?"

"Even Aunt Amie," he said.

"We're going to try and catch whoever's making the threats," Ryan said.

"Quiet, boy," Cinch interrupted. "You're spilling the beans."

"Come sit down," Uncle Matt said. He pulled a chair around and put it in Aunt Amie's place at the open end of the table.

"I think we've figured out a way so that you can safely solve this mystery. Denise's parents have agreed," Uncle Matt said, "so if it works you're in business."

"When do we start?" Rainie asked.

"After a quick breakfast," Uncle Matt said, "and you get a quick shower and get dressed."

"Sounds good." Rainie hurried back to her room

to get ready.

After her shower she felt better, but she still couldn't get Jennifer out of her mind.

"It's about time," Uncle Matt said when she walked into the living room.

It was still dark when Rainie, Ryan, Cinch and Uncle Matt drove into the Rodriquez ranch yard. Uncle Matt parked the pickup next to Denise's truck. They got out of the pickup, and Denise came out of the house to meet them.

"Here are the keys to my truck," Denise said.

"You're not going?" Rainie asked.

"No, I've got a dentist appointment later this morning."

"I wish you could come," Rainie said.

"So do I," Denise replied. "I hope you catch them."

The eastern horizon was turning from lavender to pink when they pulled into the turnout where Denise, Kerry and Rainie had parked before.

"What if whoever has been making the threats didn't see us drive up here?" Rainie asked.

"I thought we'd spend the morning," Uncle Matt said. "Hopefully that will give them enough time to notice us."

When there was enough light to see the trail up the ridge, Cinch and Ryan stationed themselves on the top of the hill, and Rainie and Uncle Matt continued on to the cave. Uncle Matt carried the pack this time.

Rainie wondered if the plan would work. But did solving the mystery really matter now? Whoever had been chained in the cave was probably dead. What mattered now was Jennifer. What could Rainie do to help?

When Uncle Matt and Rainie reached the cave, Uncle Matt unloaded the pack.

"Here, put these on." Uncle Matt handed Rainie a dust mask and gloves. Rainie did as she was told. She felt as if she was just going through the motions. Somehow her heart didn't seem to be in it today.

Uncle Matt took off his cowboy hat and laid it on the pack. "I hope I can get through that hole," he said as he slipped the elastic band of the dust mask over his head.

"Kerry made it without any problem," Rainie said. "It's bigger than it looks. Should we check for snakes?"

Kerry had left the yucca stick laying next to the hole. Uncle Matt used the stick and probed into the hole, then threw in a few rocks. "There's nothing in there," he said. He grabbed two flashlights from the pack. "I'll let you go first, that way if I get stuck you can push me out."

"You're not going to get stuck." Rainie put the mask on and then crawled in. She leaned against the back wall and held her flashlight so that he could see to get in.

"If I eat anything while I'm in here," he joked, "I

won't be able to get out."

Rainie showed Uncle Matt where the chain was bolted into the wall.

"What else are we looking for?" Uncle Matt asked.

"Anything that may help us identify who and why the person was confined here."

Rainie started by the door entrance scanning the floor carefully; Uncle Matt searched at the other end.

"This floor is so dusty," Uncle Matt said. "I think we'll have to dig."

"Come here," Rainie said. She pointed to a break in the floor dust where she had pulled out the chain the day before. "There's a piece of yellow metal sticking up where I pulled out the end of the chain."

"Gold!" Uncle Matt said. "We've got to tell Ryan. We've found Geronimo's gold."

"Quit teasing," Rainie said.

Rainie reached down and pushed dust from around the metal object with her finger. "What do you really think it is?"

"It looks like the top of a lock," Uncle Matt responded.

Rainie brushed more dust aside until most of the lock was exposed.

"That's an old brass lock," Uncle Matt said. He picked up the lock and passed it to Rainie. Then he focused his attention back on the spot where the lock had been. "I think there's something else below the lock. Look, it's hard." He tapped it with his finger.

Rainie brushed the dust away, revealing another piece of metal, but it was much larger than the lock. A smooth black surface appeared.

Suddenly she stopped. "I don't know if we should be digging like this," Rainie said. "We might be destroying evidence."

She placed the lock back on top of the black metal and then sprinkled dust over the whole area until it was covered.

"What are you doing?" Uncle Matt asked.

"This is government land, isn't it?"

"Yes, it belongs to the Bureau of Land Management," Uncle Matt said, "but what does that have to do with anything?"

"The BLM probably has an archaeologist who could help us do this," Rainie said, "and then we could make sure we're doing this right."

"You're quite a young lady," Uncle Matt said. "I don't know many people who could stop where you just did. It's like leaving a Christmas present unopened until after Christmas. Don't you wonder what's under that lock?"

"Sure," Rainie said, "but Aunt Amie's right. I've been treating this mystery like a game. I want to make sure we are doing the right thing. And since yesterday I don't know if what happened in this cave is that important. Whoever was chained here is already dead by now."

"Let's go back outside," Uncle Matt suggested.

Rainie crawled out, and then Uncle Matt struggled through the opening.

"If you're going to get an archaeologist to help you, you better get a skinny one," Uncle Matt said. "That's a tight fit."

With the mask off Rainie could breathe better. She hadn't realized how long they'd been in there. She passed Uncle Matt's hat to him, put the flashlights back in the pack and then slipped a pack strap over one shoulder.

"We can't go back yet," Uncle Matt said. "We haven't heard anything from Ryan and Cinch."

She put the pack down and sat on the flat rock.

They sat in silence for a few moments. Finally, Rainie asked, "Could God heal a person who has AIDS?"

"I have no doubt that He could," Uncle Matt said.

"Why hasn't He healed Aunt Amie's MS?"

"Wow," Uncle Matt gasped, "no wonder you couldn't sleep last night."

"I couldn't get Jennifer out of my mind." Rainie wiped a tear from the corner of her eye. "And I keep wondering why God heals sometimes and other times He doesn't."

"I can't pretend to give you a complete answer," Uncle Matt said, "but I think I can give you one that may help. Once, when the apostle Paul was having a physical problem, he prayed three times for God to heal him. And God didn't heal him. Instead, God gave him a special message. He said,

'My grace is sufficient for you, for my power is made perfect in weakness.' "

"What does that mean?" Rainie asked.

"Let me use Aunt Amie as an example," he said. "God hasn't healed her MS, but He has given her a special grace to deal with her handicap. He's given her a writing ministry that she never had before. And you've heard her say that she wouldn't trade her wheelchair for a pair of good legs. God's done something special in her life in spite of the MS. He's demonstrating His power in her life through her MS."

"Don't you miss Africa and your work there?" Rainie asked.

"Yes, but God has given us grace to deal with that."

"Why do we anoint sick people with oil and have the elders pray over them at church?"

"Because James 5:14-16 says that's what we are supposed to do."

"Did Aunt Amie have that done?"

"Yes," Uncle Matt said, "and I believe God did something special in her life when she was prayed for by those elders. You see, Christ is our Healer. I can't heal Jennifer, but I believe Christ can. When someone comes forward in church to be anointed, I know God honors their faith. They are placing their trust in Christ to heal. I believe that when we agree together for a person to be healed, God works. He either heals the sickness or gives them special grace to deal with the illness."

"But wouldn't they rather be healed," Rainie asked, "than have grace?"

"Why don't your ask Aunt Amie that question when we get home?" Uncle Matt replied.

"Hey," Ryan called from the ridge above, "look who we caught."

Cinch and Ryan had a boy between them, and they led him down the trail toward the cave. Rainie didn't recognize him at first, but when they got closer she wasn't surprised. It was T.R. Holton. Most people called him Terror. Ryan and Rainie had had trouble with him before. Maybe he was the person who was making all the threats. But what reason would T.R. have for making those threats?

6

T.R.'s Story

Cinch and Ryan held T.R. tightly between them. T.R. still wore the same dirty black cowboy hat that he wore the day he beat up Ryan. The ugly look on his face said that he wanted to do it again.

"Turn him loose," Uncle Matt commanded as he walked toward T.R. and looked down at him. "You're not going to run away, are you?"

T.R.'s expression turned from ugly to afraid; he looked at his toes. His toughness disappeared.

"We caught him by the pickup," Ryan said.

"I wasn't doin' nothin'," T.R. sneered.

"Then what were you doing?" Rainie asked.

"I was tryin' to find out what you're doin'," he said. Then he glanced up at Rainie with an angry glare. "Why are you messin' with Uncle Gab's grave?"

"What are you talking about?" Rainie asked.

"Wait a minute," Uncle Matt said. "Who told you it was a grave?"

"My mom and my grandma." T.R. pointed toward the adobe wall. "There used to be a plastic wreath right over there."

Rainie inspected the area where T.R. had pointed. "There is a wire sticking out of the ground here."

"Cinch," directed Uncle Matt, "take Ryan, and search down the arroyo, and see if you can find the wreath T.R. is talking about."

"T.R., this isn't a grave," Rainie said as she turned toward the cave. "I'll show you."

"I'm not goin' in there." T.R. crossed himself and took off his hat and held it in his hands. "We used to come here when I was little during the fiesta and bring wildflowers. My grandma and mom would say prayers for Uncle Gabriel's soul."

Rainie felt terrible. Maybe someone had died there, but she was sure it wasn't a grave. At least, she didn't think they were buried there.

"We found it," Ryan yelled as he came running back, waving a pink and purple plastic flowered wreath.

"The rain must have washed it down there," Cinch said.

T.R. took it and attached it to the wire at the bottom middle of the wall. Then he put his hat back on. "Can I go now?"

"Not quite yet," Uncle Matt said. "When did you

first see Rainie and Denise here?"

"Yesterday," he said. "From our house I could see the pickup parked here."

That made sense, Rainie thought. The Holton ranch was the first place up the canyon from Monticello. And if T.R. was telling the truth, he probably wasn't making the threats. "We better get back to the truck," Rainie said.

"Why?" Ryan said. "I haven't gotten to look in the cave." He raced up the hillside.

"I'll tell you all about it when we get there," called Rainie. She knew that if she made her answer mysterious, Ryan wouldn't argue. He was becoming just as curious as she was.

"What was your Uncle Gab's full name?" Rainie asked T.R. as they hiked back up the trail.

"Gabriel Flores," T.R. answered. "He was my grandma's older brother. Her family was one of the first to settle in the valley."

"Do you know how your uncle died?" she asked.

"I've never heard," said T.R. "All I know is he ran the general store."

"Doesn't it seem funny to you that he would be buried up here?" she asked. "Why wouldn't they have buried him in the cemetery?"

"I never thought about it," he said. "I haven't been up here for three or four years. I'll ask my mom, but she may not know either. I'm not even sure Grandma would know."

"Is your grandma still alive?"

"She's in the nursing home in Geronimo

Springs," he replied.

"Oh no!" Ryan yelled from the hilltop.

When Rainie and T.R. joined the others on the hilltop, they were looking down at the track. Both tires on the passenger side were flat.

"I just hope someone didn't slash them," Uncle Matt said.

They scrambled down the bank to the truck.

"Somebody means business," Cinch said.

Both tires had been slashed, and in the dust on the sideboards, "We Warned You" had been scrawled.

7

Calling for Help

It took most of the afternoon for them to get back home. And if it hadn't been for T.R.'s help, it would've taken longer. For some reason T.R.'s motorcycle hadn't been bothered, so he and Ryan went for help. Rainie couldn't ever remember Uncle Matt being so upset.

"I can't believe that with all the people we had walking around up there someone could come up and do such a thing. How did they get away so fast? I just can't believe it. Cinch didn't see or hear a thing. But then—neither did I. I just can't believe it." Uncle Matt paced the floor. "If it had been my truck, it would have been different," he said.

"What are you going to do now?" Aunt Amie asked.

"Pay for Denise's tires," he said.

"I knew that," she said. "What about these guys

making the threats? It doesn't sound like they're going to quit now."

"You're right. Things are deadly serious. Who knows what they'll do next? I think they mean business, but Rainie's got a good idea," Uncle Matt said.

"I'm going to see if I can get a hold of a government archaeologist who can tell us what the cave is." She thumbed through the yellow pages.

"There's a special governmental section in the front," Uncle Matt said. "You'll have to look under United States BLM. Their district office is in Las Cruces. It might take a while to get them up here."

"Can I try?" Rainie said.

"I think your plan is better than mine," Uncle Matt said. "My bright idea sure didn't work out too well. I would imagine that whoever is making these threats wouldn't want to come up against a government agency."

Rainie spent the next half hour talking to a BLM archaeologist. She found out she had done the right thing by not disturbing any more of the cave than she had. The archaeologist was really interested, but he said it would be at least ten days before he could come up there.

When Rainie told him about the threats they had received and that she felt the situation was almost hopeless, the archaeologist informed her that he knew the U.S. Forest Service archaeologist in Geronimo Springs. Maybe the Forest Service archaeologist would save him the 200-mile round trip from Las Cruces. He took Rainie's number and said he'd have the Forest Service archaeologist call her.

It would probably take quite a while for the calls to go through. Now she just had to wait. Maybe things were going to work out. But what about Jennifer? How could things work out for her?

Rainie knocked on Aunt Amie's office door, then stuck her head around the door and asked, "Can I talk to you for a minute?"

"That's fine," Aunt Amie said. "I need a break anyway."

"Uncle Matt and I were talking this morning about Jennifer," Rainie said, "and I wanted to ask you a few questions."

"Grab a chair," said Aunt Amie as she turned her wheelchair away from her computer. Rainie moved a folding chair to face her aunt and then sat down.

"I've heard you mention several times that you wouldn't trade what God has taught you through your MS for healthy legs," Rainie stated. "What do you mean by that?"

"God has drawn me closer to Himself spiritually in spite of my MS," Aunt Amie said. "I know I was serving God before, but often I was trying to serve Him in my own strength. Now, with little physical strength, I have to depend on Him more spiritually."

"Uncle Matt said you were anointed to be healed," Rainie continued. "Why hasn't God healed you?"

"He did."

"But you're still in the wheelchair."

"In the Bible it tells us that Jesus died on the cross for our sins and our sicknesses. He died for our spiritual and physical needs. We are healed because of Christ's death on Calvary. Do you understand that?"

Rainie nodded.

"I believe God did something very special in my life even though He didn't heal my MS," Aunt Amie said. "You see, He took away fears that I have had all my life and gave me a confidence in Him that I've never had before."

"Uncle Matt called it special grace," Rainie added.

"That's right," Aunt Amie said. "Jesus told Paul, 'My grace is sufficient for you, for my power is made perfect in weakness.' "

"But how does God decide whether He is going to heal us physically or spiritually?" Rainie asked.

"Sometimes He heals both," Aunt Amie said. "He knows what we need and how we can best serve Him."

"So you believe God could heal Jennifer?" Rainie asked.

"Certainly," Aunt Amie said, "but what kind of healing does she need?"

"I see what you are trying to say," Rainie said. "She needs to be healed spiritually and physically."

"Don't discount that Jesus couldn't heal her physically first," Aunt Amie continued. "He often healed people in the Bible physically so that they would then come to know Him spiritually."

"So Jesus knows Jennifer's need," Rainie smiled and said.

"That's right," Aunt Amie said. "Why don't we pray for her now?"

Aunt Amie and Rainie had just started praying when the phone rang.

"I'll get it," Rainie said. "Hello."

"Is this Rainie Trevors?" a woman's voice asked.

"Yes, it is."

"I have a friend with the BLM who asked me to call you. My name is Lesley Van Hope. I am the district archaeologist for the Forest Service. How can I help you?"

Rainie explained the situation with the cave, and the archaeologist sounded excited about helping. The archaeologist asked Rainie if they could meet Monday morning in Monticello.

Rainie turned to Aunt Amie and held her hand over the receiver. "This is the Forest Service archaeologist. She wants to know if I can meet her in Monticello on Monday."

Aunt Amie smiled and nodded.

Rainie finished making the arrangements and then hung up.

Rainie sat back down, and she and her aunt finished praying.

"Thank you," Rainie said as she stood up.

"That's what I'm here for," Aunt Amie said.

"Do you think I could call Jennifer tonight?" Rainie asked.

"If that's what you think the Lord wants you to do," Aunt Amie replied.

"I'm sure it's what He would want me to do," Rainie said. She felt a peace for the first time in days. A peace that things would work out.

8

The Find

Monday morning, Rainie, Denise and Kerry were waiting at the Monticello town square to meet the archaeologist.

"Why'd we have to get here so early?" Kerry complained.

"Rainie is always early," Denise said.

"We're only twenty minutes early," Rainie replied. "I didn't want to take a chance of missing her."

Kerry and Denise sat on a picnic table top, and Rainie sat on a bench.

"I'm just glad you asked us to come along," Denise said, then she poked Kerry in the side with her elbow. "I'm not complaining."

"Well, you didn't have to drive all the way out here from town," Kerry complained. "I could have gotten some more sleep."

"He needs his beauty sleep," Rainie joked.

"He'd need a coma," Denise said.

Both girls laughed, and Kerry groaned.

"I quit," he said as he threw up his hands. "Two against one isn't fair."

Rainie still had a lot of questions she couldn't get out of her mind. Would their opposition try to make any more threats? What could they do next? What would the archaeologist think of the cave?

Even with all the excitement about exploring the cave with a professional, Rainie still felt preoccupied. She couldn't get Jennifer out of her mind. One question rose above the rest. Had Jennifer gone to church yesterday?

Rainie had called Jennifer on Friday night. Jennifer had been thrilled to hear from Rainie, but she remained silent when Rainie explained that she thought God could heal her.

When Rainie suggested that Jennifer go to church and be anointed for healing, Jennifer started to cry. She said no one wanted anything to do with her.

Rainie did something she'd never done before; she prayed over the phone. It felt strange, but Jennifer quit crying. When Rainie hung up, her cheeks felt wet. She hadn't even noticed her own tears. Now all she could do was pray, but she felt a peace. She knew she'd done the right thing.

A green jeep braked at the stop sign in front of the town square and then pulled over near the picnic table and parked. Rainie, Kerry and Denise stood up and walked toward the jeep.

The woman inside put her sunglasses on the dashboard. Rainie couldn't believe how young she looked. Could this be the right person? The woman opened the door and stepped out. She was wearing a green Forest Service uniform. As she walked toward them, Rainie could see that the name tag above her pocket read "Lesley Van Hope: Gila National Forest."

"I'm Lesley Van Hope," she said as she reached out to shake hands with Denise.

Denise, Kerry and Rainie introduced themselves.

"When you mentioned your name on the phone," Lesley said, looking at Rainie, "I thought I remembered your name. Didn't you girls figure out how to read some petroglyphs further up the canyon?"

Rainie nodded.

"Rainie really figured them out," Denise said. "I was just along."

"That's not true," Rainie said, "you helped too."

"So, I believe we're off to investigate some caves today. Why don't you ride with me?" Lesley said.

Rainie grabbed her pack, and they all got in the jeep.

Lesley put her sunglasses back on and then started the truck. "How far do we have to go?" she asked.

"About three-quarters of a mile," Kerry said.

"I think I know something that you may be interested in," Lesley said. "It's a Forest Service project called Passport In Time. We call it PIT for short."

"What is it?" Rainie asked.

"It's a program where volunteers are involved in an archaeological dig," Lesley stated. "We have one starting in this district in three weeks."

"Pull over in the turnout on the right." Rainie pointed ahead.

They pulled over and stopped. But no one moved.

"What's the project you're going to be excavating?" Rainie asked.

"An old ranch up by Hillsboro," Lesley said.

"Why would you do that?" Kerry asked. "I thought you'd dig up Indian ruins."

"I'm a historical archaeologist," Lesley explained. "My specialty is recorded history."

"That's why you were so interested in the cave," Rainie said.

"Excited is a better word," Lesley said. "I've never heard of a site like what you described over the phone."

Lesley opened the door and waited for the others to get out. Then she reached behind the seat and pulled out a small pack and camera case.

Kerry led them up the trail to the ridgetop. A bank of dark clouds hung ominously in the west.

"Did you close the windows of your truck?" he asked Denise.

"I think I did," Denise answered.

"You did," Rainie said.

"We may get wet before this is over," Kerry said, "if we don't get moving."

"We can wait it out in the cave," Lesley said.

"It's not very big," Rainie replied.

Rainie told Lesley about T.R.'s story as they walked down the ridge to the cave.

"I agree with you," Lesley said. "It doesn't seem likely that it would be a grave from what you've described. But you can check it out easily enough."

"How?" Rainie asked.

"The local library should have cemetery records," Lesley said. "They can tell you who was buried and where."

"That's great," Rainie exclaimed. "All we'll have to do is look for Gabriel Flores' name."

When they reached the cave, they took the dust masks and flashlights out of their packs.

"We'd better take the packs inside with us," Lesley said. "The rain's not far off."

Rainie went first, and then Kerry passed in the packs.

"Let's stay as close to the adobe wall as we can," Lesley instructed after they were all in. "I don't want us stepping on anything that might be fragile. Plus, if we don't move around too much, it'll help keep the dust down."

"We walked over most of the area the other day," Rainie said. "I hope we didn't hurt anything."

"We'll find out," Lesley said as she reached in her pack. She took out her camera and snapped several pictures of the chain attached to the wall. The camera flashes in the small room were almost blinding.

"Show me where you pulled the chain out," she said.

Rainie pointed the beam of her flashlight toward the place. "What can we do to help you?" she asked.

"Here, take one of these," Lesley said, handing Rainie a small trowel.

"I think the lock is right here." Rainie knelt and pointed with the trowel.

Lesley knelt next to Rainie and with short gentle strokes began removing dust with the trowel. Then she showed Rainie how to use the trowel.

Rainie watched closely. After a minute or so, Rainie started helping her.

"Do you always work that slow?" Kerry asked.

"Yes," Lesley said, "we have to be extremely careful."

When part of the lock was revealed, Lesley took a paintbrush and brushed the rest of the dust away. Then she stepped back and took a picture of the exposed lock.

"You didn't go any deeper than this?" Lesley asked.

"Just barely," Rainie answered. "I could see the black metal surface of something."

"Let's work out a little farther," Lesley said. "We need to level this area before we go any deeper. We don't want to miss anything."

For the next half hour, they made a two-foot square around the lock. Then they began at the edge of the square and started taking off a little dirt, a level at a time. During the process, Lesley took several notes and measurements. Soon an object about the size of a plate was revealed. Lesley brushed it clean and leveled the square all the way around it. Now the lock and the object looked like an island in the middle of the square. Then Lesley stepped back again and took another picture.

"What is it?" Denise asked.

"I think it's an old military mess kit," Lesley said.

Rainie stood and stretched. "What do we do next?" she asked.

"I don't think there's any sense in going deeper," Lesley said. "These seem to be the only things in this area." She picked up the lock and laid it on some plastic next to the square. Then she carefully picked up the mess kit and turned it over.

"Could there be something inside it?" Kerry asked.

"That's what we're going to find out," Lesley said. On the kit bottom she flipped a piece of hinged metal to the side. The kit came apart in two pieces.

"Pick up the lock and spread out the plastic some more," she directed Rainie.

After Rainie leveled and spread out the piece of plastic, Lesley laid the kit in the middle. Then she gently grabbed the kit with both hands and lifted off the top.

A folded piece of paper lay in the kit bottom.

Lesley put the kit lid down next to the bottom and took another picture.

"Now what?" Denise asked.

"We bury it again," Lesley said.

"You've got to be kidding," Kerry said.

Lesley smiled and nodded. She picked up the paper and unfolded the first fold. "There's something written in pencil on the outside."

By its size they knew it had to be a letter.

"What does it say?" Rainie asked, leaning closer.

"It's in Spanish," Lesley said, "and I can't read it."

"Denise knows Spanish," Rainie said.

"I can speak it," Denise said, "that doesn't mean I can read it."

"Please try," Kerry pleaded.

Kerry held his flashlight closer to the letter. Denise leaned over Lesley's shoulder.

"I think it says," Denise said, " 'When others will understand.' "

"Wow," Kerry said, "I can't wait to see what's inside."

"Listen," Lesley said. "It's raining. We might be stuck in here for a while."

"That's okay," Kerry said. "We're going to read the rest, aren't we?"

"First, let me get a picture of this outside note," Lesley said. "It's pretty light, I don't know if it will take." She put the letter back down in the mess kit lid, then knelt and snapped a picture.

She picked up the letter again and carefully

opened the top. She smiled and announced, "We're in luck. It's in English, and it's written in ink." Then she read the letter to them.

Oscar G. Willett
Alberton, Montana
September 20, 1917

Dear Gab,

I know you haven't heard from me since the war, and I wish I were writing under better circumstances. I've written the rest of your squad to inform them of my plight.

You remember when we were given the detail to evacuate the lepers from the battle zone in the Philippines? Somehow I must have contracted leprosy. I am now being quarantined, and I don't know what will become of me and my wife.

I hope you haven't caught it, too. I've had it for a long time and not known what it was. I just returned from Mayo Clinic in Rochester, Minnesota, where they gave me the devastating news.

I don't know what you can do if you have it. Just try to protect those around you.

Sincerely,
Oscar G. Willett

Lesley put the letter down and took a picture of it. No one said a word.

They sat with their backs against the wall and listened to the rain.

"What's leprosy?" Kerry asked.

"Well," began Lesley, "it's not a pretty disease. It attacks a person's skin and nerves and causes swelling, lumps and discolored skin. It can lead to permanent deformity. Years ago people didn't know much about it, but they feared it because of how it affected a person's appearance."

"Yeah," Rainie said. "In Bible times, lepers had to yell 'unclean' everywhere they went so that healthy people could get out of the way. No one wanted to touch them."

"Can you imagine what it must have been like to find out you were a leper?" asked Denise.

Rainie didn't need to imagine. She thought of Jennifer. Everyone sure wanted to stay out of Jennifer's way.

9

Searching for Answers

"Do you think he died in there?" Denise asked as they walked back up the trail.

"I don't think so," Lesley said. "The lock was pried off. Whoever let Gabriel go didn't have the key."

"But that doesn't prove anything!" Kerry exclaimed. "They could've pried the lock off his body."

"Then why would he have left the letter?" Rainie said. "I think we are 'the others' he was writing to who are supposed to understand. But it's all still a big mystery. What happened to him? Why was the cave bricked over?"

"I think the cave was closed off," Lesley said, "to protect other people from leprosy. Or at least that's what whoever rescued Gabriel thought. Then they made up the story about it being a grave."

"That's a nice thought," Kerry said. "We've probably been exposed to leprosy."

"I don't know much about leprosy," Lesley stated, "but one thing I know, it's not very contagious. Many doctors and nurses who have worked with lepers for years have never come down with it."

"That's a relief," Kerry said.

"I guess I'll check the cemetery records," Rainie said, "to see if I can find out what happened to him."

"Check the old newspapers, too," Lesley said. "You'll need to look for issues around the time of the letter."

"I think I'm going to try and find out what happened to Oscar Willett, too," Rainie replied. "If I call Aunt Amie, do you think we could go to the library?" Rainie asked Denise.

"If my truck is still okay," Denise said, "but I'll have to call my folks. They are terribly worried about me whenever I go anywhere without them. These deadly threats have made them awfully nervous."

Rainie had forgotten about their enemies. She hoped they hadn't struck again.

"Think about going on the PIT dig," Lesley said as she dropped them off at the town square.

Rainie, Denise and Kerry waved as she drove away.

"I can't believe the vehicles are okay," Denise

smiled and said. "I wonder why they left them alone."

"The United States government," Rainie said. "They knew they would be in real trouble. They probably don't have too much to fear from private citizens."

"Maybe they just weren't around today," Kerry said.

"He is so encouraging," Rainie teased. "Is he like this all the time?"

"Oh, this is a good day," Denise joked.

"A guy can have an opinion, can't he?" protested Kerry.

"Mrs. Hudson, we have some very important work to do at the library," Denise said with her British accent. "Could you please have tea waiting for us when we get back?"

Rainie and Denise burst out laughing and ran to Denise's pickup.

Kerry threw his hat down and then walked toward his car.

"Do you know what he said when he threw his hat down?" Rainie asked.

"Girls," Denise burst out. They laughed again.

"I'm going to check the cemetery records and newspapers," Rainie said when they entered the library.

"I'm going to check what I can find on leprosy," Denise said.

The librarian showed Rainie how to use the microfiche machine for the newspapers and how to look through the cemetery records. Denise searched the book stacks for books on leprosy.

After two hours, Rainie rescued Denise from a pile of books. "You've got to come see what I've found."

Rainie led Denise to the microfiche machine.

"What is it?" Denise asked.

"It's the *Sierra Free Press* newspaper for October 2, 1917," Rainie said. "Sit down."

Denise sat down. Rainie leaned over Denise's shoulder and pointed at the screen. "Look at the headline over this article."

" 'Monticello General Store Gutted'," Denise read.

"The store that Gabriel Flores owned mysteriously burned down," Rainie said. "They assumed he was burned in the fire because he lived in the back of the store."

"That's strange," Denise said. "If he died in a fire, how could he be buried in the cave?"

"Stranger yet," Rainie said, "there's nothing about him being buried anywhere in the cemetery records."

"Maybe the records don't go back far enough," Denise suggested.

"The records go back to the 1800s," Rainie said, "and I didn't find a thing. Did you find out anything?"

"Just that leprosy is called Hansen's Disease, and it's completely controllable by medication today," Denise said.

"Anything else?"

"Before the 1940s there was no effective treatment," Denise continued. "But the lepers—by the way, they don't like to be called lepers—didn't die of leprosy. Pneumonia used to be the biggest killer. Their resistance would get down, and they wouldn't recover from common sicknesses; plus, there were no antibiotics back then."

"That sounds a lot like the way AIDS patients die," Rainie said. "People don't die from AIDS, they die from something else because their immune system can't fight for them."

"Something else," Denise added. "They still don't know what causes leprosy, and it's not highly contagious."

"Doesn't that make you feel sick," Rainie said. "People were treated awful if they had leprosy and it wasn't even that contagious. I wonder what really happened to Gabriel Flores?"

Rainie turned off the microfiche machine, and they walked back to where Denise had been studying.

"Look," Denise said, "this wasn't here before."

Someone had placed a piece of scrap paper on the books where she had been working. "This Is Your Last Warning" was written on the scrap paper.

"Come on," Rainie yelled. The girls ran out of the library into the parking lot.

A guy with a red helmet mounted his motorcycle and jump started it. They watched as he leaned down as if he had dropped something. When he noticed the girls, he sped away.

10

T.R. Helps

"I've seen that guy before," Denise said, "but I can't remember where."

Rainie walked over to where the motorcycle had been parked. There was something blue on the pavement. It looked like a syringe.

"What are you doing?" Denise asked.

"He dropped something," Rainie replied. "Look at this."

"Are you sure you should handle that?" Denise cautioned. "That could be something from drug use!"

Rainie thought Denise might be right. Maybe the guy was a drug user. But the syringe didn't look quite right. It had a spring inside. Rainie pushed the plunger down and a pen point popped out.

"It's a pen," Rainie said. "I wonder if it's the same color that was used on the note." She passed it to Denise.

"I've never seen a pen like this," Denise said. "We could check at the office supply downtown and find out who uses a pen like this. But," she said, glancing at her watch, "it's too late today. It's already closed."

"There's one more thing we need to try to find out before we head home," Rainie said.

They both walked back inside the library.

Rainie waited at the front desk for the librarian. Denise went to collect the books she wanted to check out.

"Can I help you?" the librarian asked.

"I think it may be a long shot," Rainie said, "but I've got the name of a man that I want to research. I don't know anything about him."

"Okay. Our Insta-Facks computer might be able to help you," the librarian said. "I'll show you how to use it." She led Rainie to a computer monitor at the other end of the desk.

"What is the man's name?" the librarian asked.

"Oscar G. Willett," Rainie spelled.

The librarian typed the name on the keyboard and then pushed a button that read "Search."

A list of names appeared on the screen. The name Oscar G. Willett was lit up by the cursor. "We do have something about him in the system," the librarian said.

Just then, Denise walked up behind them. "What are you doing?" she asked.

"Looking up something on Oscar Willett," Rainie

said.

"You mean there's something in there about him?" Denise exclaimed.

"It's about to come up." The librarian hit another key. "There is a newspaper article in *The Missoulian*. We don't have the text, but I can find out what it's about."

She moved the cursor and pushed another key. "Oscar G. Willett, state senator for Mineral County, contracted leprosy and was quarantined near the town of Alberton, Montana."

"Is there any way we could get the text?" Rainie asked.

"We could fax a request for the article," the librarian said, "but it would take overnight, and it would cost two dollars a page."

"We'll do it," Denise said.

"That's Jim Holton's truck," Denise said when she drove into the Warm Springs Ranch driveway to drop off Rainie. "I wonder if T.R. is with him?"

"Maybe you should come in," Rainie suggested. "I wonder what they want?"

"T.R. must've told his dad about what we've been doing," Denise said.

We're in trouble, Rainie thought. She wished more of the mystery would come together so she could explain why they were sure the cave wasn't a grave. *Lord, help us*, she prayed.

"See you, Sherlock," Denise said when she pulled in next to the Holton truck.

"You're coming in, aren't you?" Rainie asked nervously.

Denise turned off the truck. "I wouldn't miss getting yelled at for anything."

"Come on, Watson," Rainie said. "The executioners are waiting."

Rainie dropped her pack inside the back door. The sound of laughter echoed down the hall. Rainie nudged Denise and whispered, "What's going on?"

Denise shrugged. "I better call my folks," she said and grabbed the phone in the back entry. "I'll tell them I may still be a while."

Rainie waited beside Denise as she made her call.

When she hung up, Denise gestured toward the sounds and said, "You first."

Jim Holton, T.R., Ryan and Uncle Matt were playing a board game on the dining room table when Denise and Rainie walked in.

"Here come the investigators. We were wondering when you'd get here," Uncle Matt said.

"T.R. has something to show you," Mr. Holton said.

T.R. reached down on the empty chair beside him, lifted a large Bible and put it on the table. "This is my grandmother's. There is something you need to see in it."

Rainie and Denise leaned over the table to inspect the Bible.

"How old is it?" Denise asked.

"1859," Mr. Holton answered.

T.R. opened the front and pointed to the record pages of births, deaths and marriages. Names and dates were written in faded ink and pencil.

"After you told me about the cave," T.R. said, "I remembered Grandma's Bible. Look here." He turned the page and pointed.

The name Gabriel Flores was written and next to it was a date of birth, but no date of death.

"Uncle Gab was the second oldest of nine children," T.R. said, "Grandma is the youngest. There are dates of death on all but Uncle Gab and Grandma."

"Why isn't there any date of death?" Rainie asked. "I know of at least two ways he was supposed to have died."

"I don't think that anyone knew his date of death," Mr. Holton said.

"That confirms it," Rainie said, "the cave isn't a grave."

"But why would someone make up that story?" Denise asked.

"That's what *we* want to know," T.R. said.

"I think I can give you part of the answer," Rainie said. Then she told them about the things they'd discovered that day.

"Uncle Gab was a leper!" T.R. burst out.

"It looks that way," Rainie said, "but we'll know more tomorrow." Then she told them about the Oscar Willett article. "I think whatever happened to Oscar Willett also happened to your Uncle Gab."

"Can I help you tomorrow?" T.R. asked.

"You might be able to help even more now," Uncle Matt said. "Could there be anyone of your relatives who might be making these threats?"

"That's a good possibility," Mr. Holton said. "My wife's family is huge. All you have to do is look at the records inside that Bible and you'll see."

"I've got an idea," Rainie said, "and I'm sure we could use T.R. and Ryan's help."

"Another trap?" Ryan asked.

Rainie smiled and nodded.

"I hope it works better than Uncle Matt's," Ryan teased.

Everyone laughed.

11

More Trouble

$\mathcal{R}$ainie, Ryan, Denise and T.R. waited in Denise's truck for the library to open.

"What do you want us to do?" Ryan asked.

"Stay by the front windows in the reading area," Rainie said. "Pretend to read newspapers or magazines, but keep your eyes on the parking lot. They might try to do something to the truck again."

"You really think one of my relatives is involved?" T.R. asked.

"That's why you're along," Denise said. "I thought I recognized the guy on the motorcycle yesterday. I'm sure I've seen him in the Monticello or Winston area before."

"Somebody went in the front door," Ryan said. "It must be open."

Rainie and Denise went directly to the front

desk. Ryan and T.R. stationed themselves in the reading area.

The librarian grabbed some papers from under the counter and laid them on the desk in front of Rainie and Denise. "There are three pages," the librarian said, "and that will be six dollars."

"We really appreciate this," Rainie said as she paid the librarian.

She took the papers and walked through the reading area where Ryan and T.R. were talking rather loudly. An older man was trying to read a newspaper across from them. She could tell that he was annoyed.

"We'll be at the table on the other side of this book stack," she whispered. "Talk quieter." All they needed right now, she thought, was for Ryan and T.R. to get kicked out of the library for being too noisy.

Rainie and Denise sat down and put the papers between them on the table.

The article, dated Sunday, February 10, 1985, was from a newspaper called *The Missoulian*. The headline read "A Career Cut Short."

Oscar Willett was the first senator for Mineral County in Montana. In his second term, the headlines in the local paper on October 18, 1917, announced, "Leprosy!" The article read:

> Alberton is in a panic! The little town is like a stricken village. Shunned by his frightened friends and neighbors, a prisoner

in his own home, Oscar G. Willett faces the horror of a leper's lingering death. The fate that has come upon its leading citizen weighs visibly on the town.

Willett was pronounced a leper last month by more than a score of doctors who examined him at Mayo Clinic in Rochester, Minnesota. Yet he was allowed to return to Montana and go absolutely free until Gov. S.V. Stewart was informed of the case.

In the jungle of the Philippines, while fighting in the American Army, Sen. Willett contracted the ghastly disease. He did not discover the nature of his malady until recently, although he has been troubled with the malady for a long time.

Last winter, however, during the session of the Legislature, Sen. Willett was troubled by a mysterious ailment. He sought in vain for a cure and went finally to Rochester where he was told the truth.

The Missoulian article continued:

Willett and his wife were quarantined in their Alberton home while local and state authorities wrestled with the problem of what to do with him. An application to place him in a California leprosarium was turned down. Eventually the state built a small, nice home for him between the railroad track and the river. It was surrounded by double-thick, high barbed wire—no one was allowed in.

They had a phone to connect with the store, and their groceries were delivered outside the fence. The mailbox was over a dish of formaldehyde, and the letters had perforated envelopes so the fumes could get inside.

They lived there until the early 1920s. Then a train was halted opposite the enclosure, and they boarded a coach which was restricted to everyone but them. After several days of traveling, the couple arrived at a leprosarium at Carville, Louisiana. Willett died there on January 10, 1928, after harboring the disease for twenty-six years. His wife Elsie remained untouched by the disease and moved to Idaho.

The nice buildings where the Willetts lived in Alberton mysteriously burned down.

"How awful," Denise exclaimed.

Rainie felt sick. As she read the article she couldn't help but think of Jennifer. It wasn't Jennifer's fault that she had HIV. It wasn't Oscar Willett's fault that he had leprosy. Yet both were treated like animals. No one knew what to do with them. Rainie prayed again that God would heal Jennifer.

"I wonder," said Denise, "if we knew the truth about Gabriel Flores, would his story would be just as sad?"

"Probably a lot worse," Rainie said as she wiped a tear from the corner of her eye. "Oscar Willett was a state senator. Gabriel Flores was just a store owner."

"Why are you crying? What's wrong?" Denise asked.

"Oh," sighed Rainie, "this story bothered me because it reminded me of someone else." Rainie lowered her head so that people couldn't see that she was crying. Then she told Denise about Jennifer.

"I'm so sorry," Denise said and put her hand on Rainie's arm.

Rainie wiped her eyes with the backs of her hands and then looked up and tried to smile. She noticed Denise's eyes looked wet, too.

"I just remembered something," Denise said. "I read about that leprosarium at Carville, Louisiana yesterday. I think it's still in operation. What if Gabriel Flores was also sent there?"

"Good work, Watson," Rainie said. "Let's check the Insta-Facks computer. Maybe it can tell us something about Carville."

Rainie and Denise almost ran to the computer terminal. Rainie typed "Carville, Louisiana," and then pressed the "Search" button. Nothing came up. Then she typed in "leprosy," and when she pressed "Search," a column of related information appeared. She moved the cursor down to leprosariums and pushed "Enter."

An article by the American Medical Association told them what they wanted to know.

The hospital was still in operation under the United States Bureau of Prisons and the Public Health Service. It opened in 1894 as the Louisiana Leper home and housed up to 400 patients. Today, fewer than 170 remained, most being elderly (average age 67) who had spent most of their lives at Carville and were no longer able to function on their own.

"I can't believe it's still operating," Denise said.

"Those poor people," Rainie added.

Ryan almost collided with them as they walked back to the table. "Someone just stopped by Denise's pickup."

They ran to the reading area and looked out the windows, but there was no one by the truck.

T.R. sat with his head in his hands.

"It was my cousin Miguel," T.R. said. "He threw a black bag in the back of Denise's pickup."

12

Putting Two and Two . . .

"I wonder what's in the black bag?" Ryan asked.

"Let's go find out," T.R. replied.

"Wait," Rainie said, "maybe we should call the police."

"No," T.R. said, "he's my cousin."

"But it could be something dangerous. Look at what he did to my truck," Denise said, "and besides that, he's been making all kinds of threats."

"Who knows what he's done now!" Rainie exclaimed. "Maybe he's decided to really hurt us this time."

"Look," Ryan yelled as he pointed to an elderly man who had just pulled his car in next to the pickup.

As the man got out of his car, his hand went immediately to his face. He glanced at the back of

Denise's truck and then hurried toward the library. He held his hand over his nose and mouth until he reached the library entrance.

The kids were at the door to meet him.

"Phew. Something died out there in the parking lot," the man said. "It smells like a skunk."

"Come on," Rainie said.

They followed her out toward the pickup, but they didn't even get close. The smell was awful.

"What are we going to do?" Denise asked.

"Let's tell the librarian," Rainie replied.

The librarian called the city animal control after Rainie told her what happened. The kids waited by the window for about fifteen minutes until the animal control officer drove up.

They met the officer at the curb as he got out of his truck. "Where's the dead skunk?" he asked.

"I think it's in the back of my truck," Denise said.

The officer put a mask over his mouth and nose, then he took out a pole with a long loop on the end of it. "You'd better wait inside," he said.

The kids went back by the front windows and waited. The officer grabbed the bag with the pole and loop, put the smelly bundle in a metal box in back of his truck, and closed the lid. Then he came back in the library.

"Look's like someone found a road kill and decided to pull a prank," the officer said. "Do you know who did it?"

"My cousin," T.R. said.

"Should we call the police?" Rainie asked. "What

would the police do?"

"Probably not a lot," the officer said. "It's called malicious mischief, and it's not considered that serious a crime. No one has been hurt, no property has been damaged. There's just not much they can do."

"Well, thanks," Rainie said. "Thanks for delivering us from the skunk."

After the animal control officer left, Denise turned to Rainie and said, "Now we can check about that weird pen. Someone at the office supply ought to know who uses this kind of pen."

"I think I'm going to stay here and look over the article again," Rainie said. "Why don't you pick me up on your way back?"

"We'll go with Denise. Right, T.R.?" Ryan said.

T.R. nodded.

Denise and the guys left to check about the syringe pen.

Rainie returned to the table and read over the article again, but she didn't get any good ideas. She read it more slowly this time.

Oscar Willett was confined by the city and state governments, she noted. But who chained up Gabriel Flores? Who else knew that he had leprosy? If the public had known, it would have been in the newspaper. There would have been a panic in Monticello just like there had been in Alberton, Montana.

At least two people knew that Gabriel had leprosy, Gabriel himself and whoever walled in the cave. And whoever walled in the cave made up the story about it being a grave.

Someone else knew and helped Gabriel. But who? T.R.'s grandma didn't know, because she thought the cave was a grave.

Then Rainie remembered the story from *Old Yeller* about the man who had rabies. He chained himself to a pole.

What if Gabriel Flores burned his own store and chained himself in the cave to protect his family and the community? He didn't want a panic. The fear of a public outcry could have caused him to do anything. Most of all, he would want to protect his family. Plus, the letter from Oscar Willett had warned Gabriel, ". . . try to protect those around you."

Wait, Rainie thought. She knew how to prove that Gabriel had locked himself in the cave. But they would have to go back to the cave one last time. She'd call Lesley and share what she had learned. Maybe Lesley could meet them.

13

Shovel Test Find

"This is incredible," Lesley said as she read the Oscar Willett article. "I've never seen anything like it."

Lesley had met Rainie and the others at the Monticello town square. Now they discussed what to do next.

"I can only help you for a couple of hours," Lesley said as she passed the article back to Rainie. "I have a meeting this evening."

Rainie outlined what she had figured out that morning.

"I brought a metal detector," Lesley said. "We may need it. Let's go see what we can find."

When they reached the ridge above Monticello, T.R. and Ryan stayed behind to guard the trucks. Rainie, Denise and Lesley continued on to the cave.

"How do you know he burned his store and then locked himself in the cave?" Denise asked once they reached the area in front of the cave.

"First, whoever rescued Gabriel had to pry the lock off." Rainie said. "That means he didn't have the key to unlock himself."

"Maybe someone else locked him up here," Denise said, "like we thought at first."

"I think there were only two people who knew about his leprosy," Rainie said. "Gabriel and his rescuer."

"But what if there was a third person," Denise persisted, "like the person who locked him up?"

"You could be right," Rainie said, "but if there had been that many people knowing about it, I don't know how it would have stayed out of the newspaper, especially in such a small town. That third person probably would have told other people. He or she probably wouldn't have protected Gabriel. I think Gabriel burned his store so everyone would think he died in the fire."

"He also did it to protect his family and friends," Lesley said. "If they had found out about his leprosy, they would have burned it for him. It would've been another Oscar Willett story."

"Well, how do you expect to prove anything?" Denise asked.

Rainie pointed at the metal detector in Lesley's hands.

"What we are going to do is called a shovel test," Lesley said. "If we find something, we will first map where it is in relation to the cave. Then we will dig just a shovel blade deep and sift that shovelful through a screen."

Lesley put on the earphones and swept the detector slowly along in front of the cave. She let the flying saucer-shaped head of the detector hover barely above the ground. Whenever it beeped, Lesley mapped the position, then Denise dug a shovel test hole, and Rainie sifted the soil from the hole. Before they were finished in the area, Lesley passed the detector over the area where they'd dug to make sure they hadn't missed anything. They found rusty nails, several horseshoes and lots of rusty cans.

They worked the area systematically, moving down the arroyo, weaving in and out between the mesquite and greasewood bushes.

Lesley looked at her wristwatch. "I can only stay about another half hour."

Help us, Lord, Rainie prayed.

The detector beeped again. They dug up another nail at the base of a greasewood bush. Then it beeped again. There was something else in the same area.

Rainie whooped when a brass key came out in the screen.

"What's so important about finding that key?" Denise asked.

"Don't you see?" Rainie grinned. "He locked himself up and then threw the key away. That's why his rescuer had to pry the lock off."

"But who was the rescuer?" Denise asked.

"Someone who wanted to protect Gabriel," Rainie said, "but other than that we may never know."

"We'd better head back," Lesley said.

"What do you think about my calling the leprosarium in Carville, Louisiana?" Rainie asked Lesley as they hiked back to the trucks. "The rescuer might have been able to get Gabriel there."

"That may be the only way to track him down," Lesley said. "We know from the article that the leprosarium in California wasn't taking applications. If Oscar Willett was turned down, Gabriel didn't have a chance to get in."

"I wonder how he got to Carville," Rainie thought out loud.

"When I was reading those books about leprosy," Denise explained, "I read that there was a system for smuggling lepers into the leprosariums so that the general public didn't know. They often changed the individuals' names so they could be transported without fear of being discovered."

"I hope they didn't change Gabriel's name," Rainie said, "because we'll never solve this mystery if they did."

The next morning Rainie began at 7:30 trying to reach the leprosarium in Carville, Louisiana. It took several calls to the information operators before she was able to get the phone number.

Rainie prayed before she dialed Carville. This has to be the answer, she thought. When she reached Carville, she had to tell her story twice, then she was finally transferred to the records department. But they told her it would take a while to look up the information. If she would call back in an hour, they would have the answer for her.

The next hour seemed to last forever. Rainie did the breakfast dishes, folded laundry and wandered around the house, pausing to look at the clock every few minutes. Finally the hour was up. She got her pencil and paper ready and put it next to the phone.

Rainie dialed again and then held her breath once she reached the records department. She wrote the information down and calmly hung up the phone. With her hand still resting on top of the receiver, she yelled, "Praise the Lord!" She felt weird rejoicing over the news of someone's death. But now she knew. Gabriel Flores had died there, in the leprosarium, on January 21, 1930.

14

Fist Fight

Rainie called Denise and T.R. and told them the news about Gabriel's death. They agreed to meet for lunch at T.R.'s house, because T.R. wanted Rainie to share the news with his grandma.

"You won't believe what I discovered," Denise said when Rainie climbed in the pickup. "I found out about the pen."

"How'd you find that out?" Rainie asked.

"My mom had an allergic reaction last spring and had to go to the emergency room in Geronimo Springs," Denise explained. "She said one of the nurses in the E.R. had a pen like this."

"I wonder if Miguel Flores might be a nurse," Rainie said.

"We'll have to ask T.R." Denise replied.

During lunch Rainie told the Holtons about

Gabriel Flores.

"I'm glad we finally know the truth about Uncle Gab," Mrs. Holton said. "I always felt strange taking flowers up to that cave during the fiesta. Mother always said that it was the right thing to do. But she wouldn't say why we did it."

"She must have been real young when all this happened," Rainie said. "Do you think she could be the rescuer?"

"No," Mrs. Holton said, "she's insisted for as long as I can remember that we visit Uncle Gab's grave. We would still be doing it if she wasn't in the nursing home."

"Don't you think we should tell Grandma what Rainie found out?" T.R. asked.

"I'm not sure she'll want to know," Mrs. Holton said, "but it'll depend on if she's having a good day. Some days she doesn't seem to know what's going on anymore."

"Oh, I almost forgot," Rainie said. "Do you know where Miguel works?"

"He works at the nursing home," Mrs. Holton said, "with his brother Thomas. Thomas is an L.P.N.—licensed practical nurse—and Miguel is an orderly."

"That sounds like trouble," Denise said.

"I wish your mom didn't have to help your dad this afternoon," Denise said, as she drove with T.R. and Rainie through Geronimo Springs.

"Don't worry," T.R. said. "I'll talk to Miguel."

"I hope he'll listen!" Rainie exclaimed. "He hasn't been very reasonable so far."

"But he thought you were grave robbers," T.R. said. "What if you thought someone was messing around your uncle's grave?"

"I guess I'd be upset," Rainie said, "but I wouldn't go around making threats."

"You'd have to know Miguel," T.R. said, "to understand him."

"Do you think your grandma will remember back to when your Uncle Gab's store burned?" Rainie asked.

"She remembers the past a lot better than the present," T.R. said. "Mom says sometimes Grandma can't remember what they talk about from one visit to the next."

Kerry was waiting in his car when Rainie, Denise and T.R. drove in the nursing home parking lot. Denise had called and told him everything they'd discovered. She also thought he'd be good to have along for protection.

"I'd better go ahead and talk to Miguel," T.R. said.

The other three leaned against the side of Kerry's car while they waited for word from T.R.

T.R. got no farther than the grass next to the entrance. A man in a white uniform burst out the door and threw T.R. in the grass and pounced on him.

Kerry ran to rescue T.R., and the girls followed.

"I'll teach you," the man yelled, waving his fist

in the air.

"I didn't do anything, Miguel," T.R. yelled.

"You let those creeps desecrate Uncle Gab's grave," Miguel yelled as his open hand swept down toward T.R.'s face. T.R. turned his face into the grass and the blow landed on the back of T.R.'s head.

"Leave him alone," Kerry said.

Miguel shoved T.R.'s face in the grass again and then turned to face Kerry.

Kerry stood a head taller than Miguel, but Miguel's muscular frame made Rainie worry.

"You don't understand," Rainie pleaded. "We found out the truth about the cave. Won't you listen?"

"I'm going to teach you kids a lesson you'll never forget," Miguel sneered as he stepped toward Kerry.

Kerry clenched his fists. He looked as if he was ready for the challenge.

Miguel leaped for Kerry, but in a flash, another white-uniformed man jumped between them and tackled Miguel.

"Get him, Thomas," T.R. yelled as Miguel and the other man rolled in the grass.

"Cool down," Thomas commanded as he held Miguel down. "The rest of you better leave."

"We need to talk with you," Rainie pleaded. "Please listen to us. We know the truth about the cave. It's not a grave."

"Don't listen to them," Miguel said. "They've already poisoned T.R. They're nothing but low down, cheap grave robbers."

Miguel glared at them while he clenched and reclenched his fists. But at least he stood still.

"My mom told them to come," T.R. said as he brushed grass from his hair. "She believes them."

"Maybe we should talk," Thomas said as he glanced at Miguel. He stood between Miguel and the others in an effort to protect them. Both their white uniforms were spotted with grass stains.

Everyone was silent as they waited for Miguel's reaction.

"You're not lying?" Miguel angrily asked T.R.

"No," T.R. said, "Mom really sent us. She thinks Grandma should know the truth."

Miguel did nothing, but he seemed to be thinking.

Rainie, Denise, and Kerry took the opportunity to escape by opening the door and walking into the nursing home. Thomas and Miguel followed.

Two old men in wheelchairs were sitting by the entry window.

"Could you do that again, Thomas?" one of the men asked. "Brady was asleep, and he missed the show."

"Sorry, Joe," Thomas said as he looked at Miguel. "We don't plan on doing that again for a long time."

"But that was better than anything we see in the TV lounge," Joe said.

Everyone laughed except Miguel.

15

The Truth

The antiseptic smell bothered Rainie. She associated it with hospitals. That smell had been in the hospital where her grandfather died when she was eight. The smell brought back unpleasant memories. She still remembered how upset her mom had been.

Thomas led them through the entry, and they turned left down a hall. Older people with walkers and wheelchairs toddled down the hall. One man balanced against the hall rail, then shuffled down the hall with one hand always on the rail.

They turned right and walked down another hall. Several women sat in wheelchairs outside their rooms. They greeted the kids cheerfully as they passed. Thomas stopped and visited for a moment with each woman, then started down the hall again.

Miguel hung back. Rainie kept looking over her

shoulder to make sure he was just following and not planning any more nasty stunts.

"I don't think he'll cause any more trouble," T.R. said. "He feels pretty bad about what he's done."

Thomas stopped at the end of the hall and knocked on a door. The name plaque next to the door read "Juanita Alvarez." They could hear music from a TV game show coming from the room.

"Come in," a high, sweet voice called.

"Aunt Juanita," Thomas said, "I've brought some people I want you to meet."

Juanita Alvarez sat in a wheelchair about four feet from the TV. Her thick glasses rested on the end of her nose. Her gray hair was pulled back in a tight bun. Rainie couldn't believe how small she was. Her gray head barely rose above the wheelchair back.

She looked up at Thomas with a warm smile. Thomas introduced Kerry, Denise and Rainie.

"These are my friends," T.R. said as he knelt next to his grandma. "We've found out some things about Uncle Gabriel."

"What could you find out about Gabriel?" she asked. She touched the TV remote to turn off the TV. "He's been dead over seventy years."

Rainie, Kerry, and Denise sat on the edge of the bed. Thomas and Miguel stood near the doorway.

"Remember the cave? Are you sure Gabriel's body was in the cave?" Rainie asked.

"I don't understand what you're asking," Mrs. Alvarez said.

Rainie told her all about what they'd discovered.

Mrs. Alvarez pulled a handkerchief from her dress pocket and touched the corners of her eyes as Rainie told the story.

"See," Miguel said, "I knew this would upset her."

"Let Rainie finish," Thomas replied. "We need to know the truth."

"I believe someone helped Gabriel get to the leprosarium in Carville, Louisiana," Rainie explained. "He died there January 21, 1930. Do you know who might have helped him?"

"He was almost thirty years older than I was," Mrs. Alvarez said as she took off her glasses and wiped the lenses with the handkerchief. "I was a surprise." She tried to smile at them. Then she put her glasses back on.

"I was nine when Gabriel's store burned. I really missed him because he used to give me candy when I swept the store. Three days after the fire, I was playing in the hills when I found the cave. Gabriel was lying still. I thought he was dead. But then he heard me and rolled over. It scared me so bad I screamed. He groaned and asked for water. Then I ran to Father for help. He told me Gabriel died there. That's why he sealed up the cave."

"Do you think your father helped Gabriel get to Carville?" Rainie asked.

"He would have done anything for Gabriel," Mrs. Alvarez said as another tear rolled down her cheek. "He was never the same after Gabriel's death."

"Didn't you wonder about the store burning when you found Gabriel?" Rainie asked.

"I was too young," Mrs. Alvarez said. She put the handkerchief to her face and cried again.

"We're sorry, Grandma," T.R. said as he put his hand on her shoulder, "but we thought you should know the truth."

Mrs. Alvarez put the handkerchief in her lap and then reached out to Rainie. Rainie knelt next to T.R. and took her hand. "Thank you," Mrs. Alvarez said, "I'm glad you told me. I'm sure all you've done wasn't easy."

"No, it wasn't," Thomas said, looking at Miguel.

Rainie hadn't mentioned anything about the threats to Mrs. Alvarez.

"It was nice to meet you," Rainie said as they turned to leave.

"Come see me again," Mrs. Alvarez replied. "And thank the arche . . ."

"Archaeologist," T.R. said.

"Yes, please thank her for me," Mrs. Alvarez smiled and said.

When they stepped outside the door, Denise turned to Miguel and held out the syringe pen, "I think this is yours."

Miguel took it and looked down. "I'm sorry. I'll pay for all the damage. I didn't understand what you were doing."

"Would you really have followed through on the threats?" Rainie asked.

"I don't think so," Miguel said. "I was just trying to scare you. I couldn't believe you didn't quit."

"I'm glad she didn't," Thomas said. He shook Rainie's hand. "Well, Miguel," he said, "we'd better get back to work." He looked at the others and added, "We'll see you around." Then he and Miguel left.

"I'm sorry this is all over," T.R. said.

"It's not over," Denise teased, "not with Sherlock around. We were looking for what causes the Monticello light when we found the cave."

"Thanks for the reminder, Dr. Watson," Rainie said with her British accent. "Let's get back to work."

Denise turned toward Kerry, "Are you coming, Mrs. Hudson?"

The girls spun and walked out the front doors of the nursing home, leaving the guys behind.

"What are they talking about?" T.R. asked.

"They've been teasing me about being Mrs. Hudson," Kerry said.

"Who's that?" T.R. asked.

"Sherlock Holmes' housekeeper," Kerry replied.

"I better read *The Adventures of Sherlock Holmes* if I'm going to hang around you guys," T.R. said.

"Why?" Kerry asked.

"I'd rather choose my own name," T.R. laughed. He called, "Come on, Mrs. Hudson," as he ran to catch up with the girls.

"You'd better hope Sherlock didn't have a dog," Kerry called after T.R. as he ran to join the others.

16

Great News

Ten days later, Rainie and Ryan waited with Uncle Matt in the Albuquerque International Airport for their mom's plane. Her flight was already late.

Uncle Matt read a newspaper, and Ryan played his video game. It was the first time in the six weeks they'd been in New Mexico that Ryan had played the game.

Her mother's flight delay had cooled down Rainie's excitement. Rainie couldn't wait to hear about Jennifer. Jennifer had written the week before. She had been anointed for healing two Sundays ago, plus she'd accepted the Lord.

Rainie had mixed feelings now. The thought of living in New Mexico thrilled her, but to leave Jennifer when she really needed a friend bothered Rainie. She felt guilty that she hadn't missed Jen-

nifer until she heard that Jennifer had the HIV.
Now every time she thought of Jennifer she
remembered the sad story of Gabriel Flores. Rainie
wasn't going to let the HIV stop Jennifer from
having friends. She would continue to be
Jennifer's friend, and she would try to convince
others to be friends with her also.

If Rainie and Ryan's mom got the nursing job at
the Geronimo Springs hospital, they wouldn't
have to leave Uncle Matt and Aunt Amie. Rainie
had grown up so much in the last six weeks that
she didn't even want to contemplate leaving. Besides, if Rainie's mom got the job, Rainie might be
able to go on the Passport In Time archaeological
dig. Lesley had invited Denise and Rainie to par-
ticipate in the dig. Just the thought gave Rainie
hope that there might be another mystery close at
hand.

"I think that's Mom's plane," Ryan said and
pointed to a jet taxiing toward the terminal.

The announcement of the flight number over the
terminal intercom confirmed that it was their
mother's flight.

People started moving to the arrival area. Ryan
and Rainie walked to where they had a clear view
of the unloading tunnel.

Rainie enjoyed watching the reunions of family
and friends as passengers exited the tunnel. She
couldn't wait to see Mom.

"There she is," Ryan exclaimed as he pointed.

Rainie and Ryan ran to greet her.

She hugged them. "I've missed you so much." She had tears in her eyes.

Ryan took her bag, and Uncle Matt joined them. She hugged Uncle Matt and then turned to Rainie. "You're not going to believe what has happened. Jennifer has had two negative tests in a row. No sign of HIV. It looks like the Lord has healed her."

"Praise God," Uncle Matt said.

Rainie felt like she was going to burst with joy. She hugged her mom. How could life get any better than this? "Thank You, Jesus," she said. "Thank You."

Glossary

adobe—a brick or building material of sun-dried earth and straw; a heavy clay used in making adobe bricks; a structure made of adobe bricks.

AIDS (Acquired Immune Deficiency Syndrome)— a serious disorder of the body's defenses against disease that eventually leads to death.

arroyo—a deep, dry gully in a dry area that usually only fills with water after a recent rain.

formaldehyde—a strong-smelling, colorless liquid that is used as a disinfectant and preservative.

greasewood—a low, stiff shrub.

HIV (Human Immunodeficiency Virus)—the virus that causes AIDS by attacking the white blood cells which are an important part of the body's immune system. The virus is not highly contagious and must be passed through direct contact with blood and other body fluids.

immune system—the body's system for attacking invading viruses and bacteria. It helps to keep us free of disease.

leprosarium—a hospital for lepers.

leprosy—a disease that effects the skin and nerves causing discoloration, lumps, loss of feeling and possible deformity. Because a person with leprosy feels little or no pain, especially in their extremities, they easily injure themselves sometimes causing great harm.

malady—any sickness or disease.

mesquite—a spiny, deep-rooted tree or shrub that forms in extensive thickets, bears pods rich in sugar and is important as livestock feed.

orderly—a hospital worker who does basic jobs such as cleaning, carrying supplies and moving patients.

quarantine—to separate a sick person from others as a precaution to stop the spread of a contagious disease.

yucca—a plant with long, stiff, pointed leaves. It bears a group of white blossoms on a tall, thick stem.